SIDETRACKED

orca sports

SIDETRACKED

DEB LOUGHEAD

ORCA BOOK PUBLISHERS

Library and Archives Canada Cataloguing in Publication

Loughead, Deb, 1955-
Sidetracked / Deb Loughead.
(Orca sports)

Issued also in electronic formats.
ISBN 978-1-4598-0250-6

I. Title. II. Series: Orca sports
PS8573.08633S53 2012   jc813'.54   C2012-902831-2

First published in the United States, 2012
Library of Congress Control Number: 2012938314

Summary: Maddy's track team struggles to stay focused
after a theft and a bullying incident occur.

MIX
Paper from
responsible sources
FSC® C004071

ANCIENT FOREST ™
FRIENDLY

*Orca Book Publishers is dedicated to preserving the environment and has
printed this book on Forest Stewardship Council® certified paper.*

Orca Book Publishers gratefully acknowledges the support for its publishing
programs provided by the following agencies: the Government of Canada
through the Canada Book Fund and the Canada Council for the Arts, and the
Province of British Columbia through the BC Arts Council and
the Book Publishing Tax Credit.

Cover photography by Corbis
Author photo by Steve Loughead

ORCA BOOK PUBLISHERS   ORCA BOOK PUBLISHERS
PO Box 5626, Stn. B   PO Box 468
Victoria, BC Canada   Custer, WA USA
V8R 6S4   98240-0468

www.orcabook.com
Printed and bound in Canada.

15 14 13 12 • 4 3 2 1

For Barbara Gooch,
my friend since grade ten

chapter one

My foot is tucked up against the starting block. I'm crouched into position, waiting to hear the starter pistol go off. It's like a signal for my body. It's what triggers the rush. Beside me, Kat Jennings is crouched in the same position. She's good. And she's also my biggest rival at Eastwood High.

She has the same look on her face she always does before a race. Total focus, just like me. It's what a runner needs that split second before the race begins. You have to block out everything except your goal to cross the finish line first. In a 100-meter sprint, there's no room for error.

All eight runners are poised for takeoff. I can almost taste the tension. Our track coach raises his arm in the air. The other coaches are watching too.

"Runners, take your marks!"

There's the slightest shift along the starting line. Each grade-nine girl settles into a perfect four-point takeoff stance.

"Set!"

The muscles in my legs are like an elastic band about to snap.

Bang!

The elastic snaps, and everything is blank except my goal. I launch straight ahead, staying between the two lines that mark my lane. The only sounds are is cleats hitting the track's gritty surface. Kat and I are neck and neck. I don't care about anyone else, because we're slightly ahead of everyone. A little over twelve seconds later, Kat and I cross the finish line, practically shoulder to shoulder. Coach Reeves grins and shakes his head.

"What is it with you two anyway?" he calls out.

Kat and I are grinning too. We high-five each other, as we do at the end of every race. Not only is Kat my biggest rival, she's also my best friend. Last year she was faster than me. This year, after a lot of practice, I've finally caught up to her. For every race she wins, I win the next one. Today I won.

These early-season track practices help our coach select the fastest runners at the bantam, junior, intermediate and senior grade levels. Our bantam relay team will be made up of the four fastest grade-nine sprinters. The fastest will represent the team in the 100-meter sprint at upcoming meets. But who that will be has yet to be decided.

Some of the other kids on the track-and-field team wander over and pat us on the back. A couple of our closest friends smile from the sidelines. Isabel and Paige graduated from Wentworth Middle School with us last year. Back in middle school, we were all on the same track team. But this year, in ninth grade at Eastwood, everything has changed.

At the end of last year's track season, our coach warned us this would happen. He said that in high school, the rules of the game change and the competition is fierce. We should expect a whole new crop of athletes to compete against for spots on the team. Eastwood has a couple of different feeder schools. The track-and-field stars from those schools all want a spot on the team. Our middle school coach knew exactly what he was talking about. So many kids who were fast last year didn't even make the cut this year.

In high school there's more competition and not just on sports teams. Over the past few months, while trying to adjust to all the new competition on the track, some of our friends have drifted off to chill with other kids. Which works for me, but not so much for some of my other friends. Nothing wrong with too many friends, is what I think. But a group of us from middle school still hangs out. There's nothing like old friends.

"Come *on*," Zenia says as she strolls up to me and Kat, still trying to catch her breath. "What are you guys putting on your Wheaties in the morning anyway?"

"I don't even eat Wheaties for breakfast," I say. "In fact, I've never even tasted them! I'm just lucky, I guess. Must be these long toothpick legs."

"Yeah, right." Zenia laughs. "I know how hard you and Kat work. It's more than luck. You two were the fastest *last* year too."

"Best friends, best runners," Kat says. "How cool is that!"

Everyone on the track-and-field team, the other coaches included, is caught up in the drama. They gather along the track whenever our coach races the grade-nine girls. And at the end of each race, everyone cracks up.

Even the girls we just beat can't help but smile. They know Kat and I will train until it kills us in order to reach the top of our game. A lot of the time, our races are almost too close to call. So we always break even. How can Coach possibly choose the top runner with those crazy odds?

Only one girl, Shauna, never cracks a smile. At the end of each race, she only ever scowls. Every day this week, she has come in third. Her bright green eyes flash disappointment. Her fair freckled skin, which practically pleads for sunscreen, has a fine sheen of sweat, even though it's not that warm for May. She wants to win badly. She reminds me of the Canadian Olympic speed skater Clara Hughes. I'm sure Clara is way nicer than this girl though!

Shauna doesn't bother talking to any of us. She just flips her thick golden-red ponytail, which she always wears with a baseball cap, and stalks off as if she's mad at the world. What is *her* problem, I can't help but think.

chapter two

Kat sidles up beside me. "Talk about a sore loser," she says and runs her fingers through her wavy black hair.

"The way things are going, Shauna will be one of the top four," I remind her. "If she makes it, then we'll all be on the same relay team together. With the vibes she's giving everyone, I don't see how that can possibly work."

"If she was as fast as her brother, our relay team would be awesome," Kat says.

Shauna's brother Justin is rocket-fast. He's the star runner on the grade-ten team and an amazing sprinter. He leaves everyone else in his dust. He's one of the fastest guys in the whole school, in fact. There's talk that he's already being scouted by American colleges. His family must be so proud. I know more than a few guys on the team who wish they could be him.

My brother Matt is on the track-and-field team too. But shot put is his sport, as well as football in the fall. He and I are almost about the same height. At five foot ten, I guess he's pretty average for a guy. I *know* I'm tall for a girl. I'm kind of long and lanky, while my brother is built like a bull. And, boy, can he ever fling a shot put. He's so focused when he's on the field. But lately I worry about what he's up to when he's *not* on the field or at home. He's been acting sketchy the last few months.

Coach Reeves wanders over to where Kat and I and the others are standing. He looks confused and shakes his head.

"What am I going to *do* with you two? Something has to change at some point. You can't *both* represent the team in the hundred meter. Who is it going to be? Kat or Maddy?"

Kat shrugs. "Guess we'll have to try again on Monday, huh, Coach?"

"Yep," I say. "Another day, another race. Or ten."

There's a smirk on Coach Reeves's face. "I get the impression you two are enjoying this." Then he shrugs. "We'll give it another try on Monday. Same time, same place. And don't wear yourselves out practicing this weekend, okay?" He wanders toward the school, still shaking his head.

"So how long are you going to keep messing with his head?" Isabel asks.

"We're not messing with his head," I say. "We never know who will win either."

"It's just not the same anymore, is it?" Paige says, her face glum. "There's so much talent here to compete with. Most of us are out of our league on the track now."

"Yeah," Zenia says. "We can't keep up to you two anymore. And Shauna's fast too. Which makes it even worse."

"But at least we're all still on a track-and-field team together this year, right?" I say.

"God, how can you always be so positive about everything?" Isabel asks.

"Really," Kat adds. "You're just one bright ray of sunlight today, aren't you, Maddy?"

"Hey, we all have our strengths," I say. "We all shine at something."

"Oh *barf*!" Paige makes a gagging sound. "Little Miss Sunshine is in the house," she says, and everyone laughs.

As we all wander back into the school to grab our stuff before heading for home, some of the guys catch up with us. Zack and Nathaniel can't stop talking about how Kat and I keep coming up with the same number of winning races. They went to Wentworth with us, and we're still a tight-knit group.

Except for our friend Carter. He hangs out with a crowd of older kids now. It's as if he's trying for a fresh start with his cool new friends in high school. Fresh doesn't mean good though. He seems to get into trouble a lot for being a goof and mouthing off. Some of the guys from last year have even tried to talk to him about it. He just laughs in their faces and calls them niner geeks. And *he's* in grade nine! It's pointless.

I take one last glance at the field before heading inside. My brother Matt hasn't shown up. He's been so distant lately. Maybe he has too much on his mind. I can hardly even look at his shot put coach, Ms. Chapman. I wish I could figure out what Matt's problem is. But it's hard when he does his best to avoid talking about anything with me.

I can still hear Paige's *Little Miss Sunshine* comment. Oh, if my friends only knew about the dark little storm cloud hanging over my home life.

chapter three

As soon as I step through the front door when I get home that afternoon, I head for the kitchen. "Hey, Abuelo! Something smells *so* good! What are you making for dinner?"

My grandfather stands at the stove, stirring something in a pot. It smells like heaven, and I know it will taste that way too. I lean in to peck him on his rough brown cheek. It's something I started to do after he moved in with us. And now it has become as much of a habit as brushing my teeth.

Abuelo moved into our cozy little bungalow when he retired from his job as a school custodian a few years ago. My abuela, my grandmother, passed away three years ago. Around the same time as my dad left. Abuelo built his own room in the basement as soon as he moved in. He's great at stuff like that.

We don't talk about those tough times. Abuelo has worked hard at getting over losing the love of his life. And my mom has worked just as hard to move on after losing our dad. For some reason, my dad wanted to go live down in Florida. Mom didn't want to, so he went by himself. Things hadn't been great between them, and it was almost a relief when the constant arguing stopped.

It made sense for Abuelo and Mom to pool their resources. And I think they're both happier helping each other. Our mom works in a day care center and cooks a lot of the meals there. So Abuelo has taken over the cooking at home.

"Is Matt home yet?" I ask, and Abuelo shakes his head.

"No, he had track practice, Madina. Didn't you see him there?"

"Oh yeah." I try to laugh, but it almost makes me choke.

"And how was track practice anyway?" Abuelo asks. "Did you win today?" His dark eyes are bright. He loves that my brother and I are part of the track-and-field team.

"Yes, I won, Abuelo. But we're still not certain who'll run the hundred meter yet. Kat and I are both top runners though. So we'll be on the bantam relay team for sure."

That makes my grandfather smile. He is so supportive. He comes to our meets sometimes, sits in the stands and cheers Matt and me on. He even pays for our cell phone accounts, probably so he knows that he and Mom can always get in touch with us. Which is why it bugs me that my brother is not being where he's supposed to be. It's as if he's putting one over on our grandfather.

Matt blows in the front door and drops his backpack. He's breathless, as if he ran all the way home.

"I'm starved!" Those are the first words out of his mouth. "What's cookin', Abuelo?"

"Cabbage and chorizo," Abuelo says, smiling.

"Again?" Matt groans. "Forget it. I'm kind of in a hurry anyway. I'll just go pick up some pizza slices or something, okay?"

"But I thought you liked my cooking, Mateo," Abuelo says.

"Yeah, but you gotta try something *new* once in a while, Abuelo," Matt says, then slips down the hall to his room and shuts the door.

"Why does he wear his pants like that?" Abuelo asks. "All hanging down like he doesn't care how he looks."

I do my best to reassure him. "It's the style now. Don't worry about it. They're just pants." I give him another peck on his whiskery cheek before heading toward my own room. I stop in front of Matt's door and knock.

"*What?*" His voice is muffled and cranky.

"Can I talk to you for a sec?"

"About what?"

He is *so* frustrating these days. "Unlock your door and you'll find out, okay?"

The latch clicks and the door opens a crack.

"Why are you being such a jerk to Abuelo?" I ask. "And why did you miss practice today anyway?"

"Bite me, Maddy," Matt says and shuts the door in my face.

I can never get a straight answer from my brother anymore. Never *ever*.

He never sticks around for long on a Friday evening. So I'm not surprised when he dashes out of the house, tossing a quick goodbye over his shoulder. Not long after, our mom comes in with a couple of bags of groceries.

"Where's your brother?" she asks and looks around, as if he might be hiding somewhere.

"He told us he was going out with friends for pizza," I say, trying not to meet her eyes.

"Oh, that Mateo loves his pizza," Mom says, flopping into a chair and kicking off her shoes. He's such a busy guy, isn't he?

He's hardly ever home now. How did track go today?"

"It went great, Mom," I say. "Kat and I still have the same problem. We always seem to break even. I win one, and then she does. If nothing changes, then Coach will have to decide for us."

"Oh, you'll see, Maddy. Something will change one of these days. It always does," Mom says. "I'd better go grab some dinner before Abuelo puts everything away."

She wanders out to the kitchen with her grocery bags. I can hear her chattering away in Spanish to my grandfather. But I'm not really listening, because I'm actually wondering if my mom could be right.

And if something really does change, will it be for good or bad?

chapter four

Ever since the snow melted and the nicer weather began after March break, Kat and I have had the same Saturday-morning routine. We meet at the school track to practice. Some of our friends head over there too. It's a good place to chill, have a few laughs and get a workout.

We have it set up with the high school, as well as with the custodian staff. They're on hand to supervise the various clubs that need to use the school on the weekend.

The drama club has weekend rehearsals for the May show, along with a glee club. And community basketball teams often use the gym for tournaments.

I make a note of who has shown up at the track. It's all the usual suspects. Keener members of the track-and-field team who feel guilty if they don't practice on the weekend. Some are kids I met when I joined the team this year. Then there are the old faces. My fellow Wentworth teammates from last year. Some of the grade-nine kids blend in easily with everyone. And then there are others who circle each other like nervous dogs sniffing out their rivals.

Zenia and some other high jumpers have already dragged out their equipment. She has to share her time between the track *and* the field now. But I know her heart is still mostly on the track. Our old teammates, Paige and Isabel, are trying to outjump each other at the long-jump pit with some of the guys.

Short- and long-distance runners warm up on the track. Kat lopes at an easy pace.

Carter runs alongside some of the new friends he's made this year. Matt isn't here. I heard him come home past his curfew. He's probably still sleeping off whatever he was up to last night.

As sprinters, our routine always starts the same. We begin with a warm-up lap. Next we follow with some stretching exercises to help loosen our joints. And then we start on our drills, which must appear totally crazy to anyone watching. We hop around like rabid bunny rabbits. It's called plyometrics, or jump training. It works for anyone who wants to increase their athletic powers. And it's actually fun too. Then right after that come the speed drills. Flat-out burning up the track in short flying bursts.

I drop my backpack in a pile with all the others under the football goalpost at the end of the field. I don't want to waste any time getting started on my warm-up. The spring sunshine beats down on my head as I lope up to my friends. It's a perfect day for training.

"Hey, Maddy," Kat says as soon as I catch up to her. "Did you sleep in this morning or what?"

"Nope, just having breakfast with my grandfather. But my brother slept in," I say as I fall in sync with her easy strides.

I fill her in about Matt missing his curfew, again, and how weird he's been acting the last few months. "I can't figure out what he's up to. He's really letting down Coach Chapman too. It's like he's hiding something. And I don't want my mom or grandfather to notice and start to worry. They have enough on their minds as it is. Why does he have to be such a jerk?"

"Brothers are good at that, aren't they?" Kat says and laughs.

"I just wish I knew what's going on with him," I say. "I can't believe how much it's bugging me. I'm starting to lose my focus on more important things, like running."

Kat stops and I almost crash into her. She puts her hands on my shoulders and stares into my eyes.

"Maddy, your brother's cool. You have to try and trust him."

"Sure hope you're right. Thanks," I say and give her a quick hug.

Nothing better than a best friend who's always there to give you a pep talk when you need one.

Kat's eyes shift toward something behind me and grow wide. "Wow," she says. "Look who's here!"

I swivel my head, and there she is. Shauna Halstead, ponytail swishing and baseball cap pulled low over her eyes. She crosses the field and starts in the direction of the track. She stares straight ahead, as if she's the only person here.

chapter five

I can't believe Shauna has actually turned up on a Saturday morning. We all know she prefers to do her training in the park so she won't have to hang out with us.

Her brother Justin has shown up too. And lo and behold, there's my brother Matt, jogging along not far behind. I can't believe he actually made it. He gives me a half wave, as if he's too cool to admit I'm related to him. The three of them drop their backpacks under the goalpost and head for the track to warm up.

Justin is broad and muscular. More than one girl looks over as he runs past us. Zenia gives him an extra-long look, which I've noticed her do before. She's so into him. With his ginger hair, he almost has a Ron Weasley look. In a second, Justin's caught up to Carter and his friends. My brother brings up the rear. Shauna starts jogging too. She doesn't bother with any of the girls from her team.

I decide I'm going to suck it up and wave at her. I start to lift my hand just as she's running past. But she looks the other way and acts as if she didn't notice my friendliness. I feel stupid, so I pretend I was scratching my head.

"Why do I even bother?" I say, more to myself than to anyone else.

"Strange girl," Kat says, watching her. "Got great form, though, doesn't she? Too bad she can't beat us, huh, Maddy? I'll bet that bugs her like crazy!" Kat grins and offers me a high five, which I return with a few misgivings.

"Too bad *I* can't beat you every time," I say.

"And too bad *I* can't beat *you* every time," Kat says. "It will all work out one way or another, don't you think? One of us will run the hundred meter, and the other will be the sub—and we'll both qualify for the relay team."

"I guess so," I say. But I don't want to mention what else I'm thinking. Which is how badly I'd like to get that spot as the top sprinter on the bantam team. What would that do to our friendship though? What if, secretly, she wants it just as badly?

And why can't I be honest about it with her? Maybe neither one of us wants to acknowledge the truth about the competitiveness between us because it could threaten our friendship?

We train past lunchtime. Shauna doesn't glance my way the whole time. She's watching her brother though. She runs with him a lot, and does her warm-ups, wind sprints and plyometrics with him and his teammates instead of with us. Sometimes it seems as if she doesn't really want to be a part of our team. If Coach Reeves announces next week that she'll be part of the relay team, I'm not sure how I'll deal with it. It sure will take a lot of energy to make it work.

Matt is pitching the shot put. A few girls stand around watching his muscles move. Some of them aren't even on the track-and-field team. I'm pretty sure they've only shown up to ogle my brother. They're purposely acting silly on the sidelines just so he'll look their way. But Matt is totally focused and just smirks and shakes his head. I'm surprised he doesn't have a girl-friend yet. Or maybe he does? Maybe that's why he's been so busy and cranky.

I don't even notice how hungry I am until one of the custodians wanders from the school. He calls out that it's nearly 2:00 and says it's time for everyone to think about putting the equipment away. In other words, he's telling us nicely to get lost.

I still have one eye on Shauna. I try to catch her attention, hoping she'll at least nod or something. It doesn't work. She doesn't seem ready to leave. As Kat and I walk away, I glance over my shoulder. She's still running on the track along with her brother, Matt and a couple of other guys. Zenia's there, too, and seems determined to try her best to make the relay team.

"I still don't get this Shauna girl," I say to Kat. "Why did she even show up if she's not interested in talking to anyone?"

"Who knows?" Kat shakes her head. "And who even cares? Why does this matter to you so much anyway? You've got me, and tons of other friends."

"I guess I just don't like it when I think someone has something against me and I don't even know why."

"It's not just you, it's *everyone*, Maddy. Anyway, if it bugs you so much, why don't you ask her? But I don't know why you'd bother," she says.

I shrug. "We're all on the same track team, you know. We'll likely even be on the same relay team with her, since she's one of the top four bantam sprinters. Look how well our team did last year. Because we were all friends, and we helped each other figure stuff out on and off the track."

Now Kat shrugs. "The rules have changed, Maddy. Everything's different this year. Way more kids, way more competition. And way more stuff to deal with. Besides, we can't be friends with *everyone*, can we?" She pauses. "So? Want to throw something together for lunch at my place? As you know, I make a mean KD with chopped-up weenies."

"How can I turn down an offer like that?" I say with a smile. I shoot one last glance over my shoulder. Shauna is staring at me. When our eyes meet, she looks away.

chapter six

All through lunch, Kat and I babble away about school stuff, and avoid the subject of who will be chosen for the girls' 100 meter. But the question hangs over our heads like a thought bubble in a comic strip. Will it be her, or me? When Kat asks for help with math, it makes for a good distraction. Poor Kat. We sit beside each other at the table, our heads together. I try to explain the Pythagorean theorem. I can tell she's totally lost by the way she stares into space instead of at the page. She's not even listening to me.

"Oh, who cares about the sides of a triangle?" she finally groans. "How is this going to matter in my life? Will you tell me, Maddy? Why do I even need to know this!"

"Well, to pass math this year, for starters," I remind her.

"Too true. I'm doomed!" Kat throws herself dramatically across the table and fake-sobs. "There's one thing for sure, Maddy," she says from under the crook of her arm. "When it comes to you and me and math, you're guaranteed to win!"

I'm not sure Kat will ever fully understand the Pythagorean theorem, even though she pretends to so we don't have to do math anymore. We check out some YouTube music videos for a while, which is a relief. It's hard explaining math to someone with a non-mathematical brain.

Afterward, I run home at a nice easy pace. Running fills me with peace and is a great stress burner. And right now, I almost wish I could run away from all the stuff that's been bugging me about my brother and Shauna, who I still can't figure out. I take a shortcut through Eastwood High and across the football field.

It's completely deserted now that everyone has gone home and the school is locked up. In fact, it kind of creeps me out. I jog along the side of the building, peering into vacant classrooms. I've almost reached the athletic field and the track when I hear a shout, and I stop.

My first instinct is to hide. My heart is hammering inside my chest, as if I've just run a race. I have a bad feeling about this. I'm almost afraid to look. Breathing hard, I back up against the school and peer around the corner.

At the other end of the field, there's some sort of scuffle going on. A bunch of guys are giving someone a hard time, pushing and shoving. Whoever is getting shoved pushes back hard. They're all so far away, I can't make out any of their faces. I glance over my shoulder. There isn't a soul in sight—nothing but the empty teachers' parking lot. The only one here to witness this is me. There's nobody to call to for help. I wish I had my cell phone, but I didn't bring it to practice today.

One of the guys is shouting. I can't hear what he's saying. The person getting bullied yells something back. I can't help but think about who was the last to leave after practice. My brother stayed behind with Shauna, Justin, a few other kids and Carter.

I press myself against the cool bricks and try to figure out what I should do. When I take another look, someone is sitting on the ground in the middle of the field as the others run off. I know what I have to do next. I have to pretend I'm just arriving. And act as if I have no clue what happened.

Why didn't I yell or call out? There's no denying I was too chicken. But now, I have to make sure this person is okay, so I sprint across the field. When I get there, I can hardly believe who it is.

"What are *you* still doing here?" is the first thing I ask Zenia.

She's sitting on the grass blinking, as if she can't believe what just happened to her.

"I wiped out on the track when I was running," Zenia says, avoiding any eye contact with me. She tries to flash one of her bright smiles as she pushes her tangled mane of sandy hair out of her eyes. I'm proud of her for sticking up for herself, but I can't tell her that.

"No way! How did *that* happen?" I try my best to sound surprised. I reach out to help her to her feet, and she slowly heaves herself up. "I was just taking a shortcut home from Kat's place. You're not hurt or anything, are you, Zenia?"

"I don't think so," she says in a dazed voice. "I just feel really stupid I let it happen. I...I guess I wasn't paying atten-tion, and I tripped over my backpack. What a total klutz!" Her eyes are locked on the direction the other kids took off in.

Zenia is totally lying. I can't believe it. She doesn't want to tell me what really happened to her. Probably because she's too proud. And I can't tell her what I saw, or she'll know I did nothing to try and help her.

"So you're going home now, right?" I say. "I'll walk with you, okay?"

"Sure, that would be cool," Zenia says.

She grabs her backpack and flings it over her muscular shoulder. Zenia works out all the time, and she's tough and wiry. She stood up to those jerks even though they completely outnumbered her. I think I know who was shoving her. I heard Carter's voice. But I don't know why it happened.

We wander home, talking about the track team and the dance coming up next Friday night. We talk about everything except what just happened to her. I can hardly concentrate on what she's saying. There's a sick knot in my gut that *isn't* from running on a full stomach.

chapter seven

On Saturday night, I stay home and try to forget the horrible scene I witnessed today. The memory of it eats away at me. Watching a *Shrek* movie with Abuelo and Mom helps. Abuelo loves the Puss-in-Boots character. He laughs at him the entire time, which makes me and Mom laugh too. My grandfather's laughing is funnier than the movie.

Of course, Matt isn't home. "Going to a buddy's place to work on an assignment," he mumbled and left before dinner late this afternoon. But I could see the lie in his shifting eyes. Why hasn't my mom figured it out, when it's so obvious?

As soon as the movie ends, Abuelo says good night and heads to bed so he can get up early to make breakfast for everyone. Now that I have a chance, I decide it's time to ask my mom about Matt. I kneel on the sofa beside her, cup her chin in my hand and look into her eyes.

"Mom, haven't you been wondering what's up with Matt lately? How come you never freak out over some of the stuff he's been doing?" I ask.

"Of course I've been wondering, Maddy. You think I should be freaking out?" Mom asks. "Why should I be freaking out?"

Is my mom totally blind, or what? "Because of the way he snaps at us all sometimes, and how he comes and goes and never really tells us what he's up to. Plus he breaks his curfew. Aren't moms supposed to worry about stuff like that?"

Mom sighs and stretches her legs. "Oh, Madina, of course I worry about your brother. All parents worry about their children. But my day starts at five thirty in the morning. I work hard with the kids at day care. My feet are always sore. And I'm exhausted when I get home. If I let myself worry about Mateo *all* the time, then I wouldn't sleep at night. I need my sleep!"

"But sometimes Matt doesn't show up for track practice," I say. "And his coach starts asking me questions I don't know how to answer."

"Sweetie, it's not your problem, is it?" Mom gently pushes my long curtain of hair behind my ear so she can see my whole face. "Your brother is sixteen now. I have to start trusting him, don't you think? I never get calls from the school. He's polite most of the time. He helps out around the house when I ask. So I let some other things go."

I smile at my mom and hope she's right about trusting Matt.

It's hard to focus on my homework on Sunday. I can't stop thinking about what I saw and how I hid. I regret doing nothing. Maybe if I'd yelled, they would have taken off sooner. Then I might actually be able to face Zenia again without feeling utterly lame.

The other thing bugging me is that my brother suddenly has an iPod! He had the earbuds plugged into his head this morning. When I asked him where it came from, he just shrugged and said he saved his allowance.

Abuelo gives us each twenty bucks a week. No way Matt could have saved enough money for an iPod. He's always got new T-shirts and hoodies. I wonder if he actually bought any of the stuff, like he said he did. It makes me queasy just thinking about how else he might have gotten these things. When I put all the pieces of the Matt puzzle together, I don't like the shape it's taking.

I can't wait for Sunday to end so I can go to school Monday and start thinking about something else for a change.

chapter eight

During the peak of track-and-field season, the coaches are relentless. They regularly call early-morning practices on top of the after-school practices. And they like to see us all out on the field by 7:30. So it's early to bed for Matt and me Sunday nights.

On Monday morning, I pound on his door at 6:45 to make sure he gets his butt moving. All I get is a growl. When I leave shortly after seven, I still can't hear my brother moving around in his room. My grandfather promises he'll get Matt up.

I let out a sigh of relief when I spot Matt loping across the field as the coaches step out of the school. I know he can be a jerk, but I don't really want him to get in trouble. Shauna and Justin showed up a couple of minutes before him. Justin gives Matt a salute, which Matt returns with a half grin and a raised eyebrow.

As soon as he reaches the track, Coach Reeves blows his whistle, and the entire team gathers around. Usually he's smiling, full of pep and armed with sayings to try and inspire us on a Monday morning.

"*Awards become corroded, friends gather no dust*," are the first words out of his mouth. His face is stony. "Anyone know who said that?"

We all stand in stunned silence. "Only one of the most brilliant American track-and-field athletes ever, Jesse Owens," he says. "Surely you know who *he* is, don't you?"

We all nod, even though I'm positive half the kids don't really know who Jesse Owens is.

"His running-broad-jump record stood for twenty-five years," says Coach. "He won four medals in the 1936 Olympics in Berlin. Do yourselves a favor and google him, okay? Anyone want to try and guess what Owens meant by that?"

We stare at the ground, our shoes and then each other. Nobody wants to meet the coach's eyes for fear he might ask them to answer. Plus he's acting pissed off about something.

"Here's a clue," he says. "It's about friendships forged on the competitive athletic field. It's about how much more important those friendships are than the actual award you win. Because that's what's important in the long run, right?"

We nod like puppets controlled by strings. Because that's exactly what we know he expects us to do.

"Yeah, that's what I thought," Coach Reeves says. "So how is it that during practice Saturday morning, when you're with friends and teammates you supposedly trust, how is it that a smartphone and an iPod can disappear from a couple of backpacks?" Coach Chapman and the assistant coaches look as pissed as Coach Reeves.

It's as if someone cracked an egg over my head and something slimy and gross is dripping down me. I review Saturday morning in my mind. Everyone left their backpacks, with water bottles and energy bars, in a heap under the goalpost. Kids wandered over now and then to grab something from their backpack, and nobody thought anything of it.

I feel sick when I glance at Zenia. She's staring at the ground. It's all starting to come together. Zenia must know who ripped off the backpacks during practice. Which is why she got pushed around on Saturday. Whoever did it wants her to keep her mouth shut about it.

"We aren't going to blame anyone or point any fingers," Coach Reeves adds.

"You know who you are, and it's up to you to make this right. Got it, everyone?"

"Got it, Coach," we murmur.

I glance around uneasily at the solemn faces to see if I can figure out who did it. If only I could get Zenia to tell me. But her mouth is a tight line. She won't be letting that information out anytime soon.

My thoughts are spinning faster and faster. I can't stop thinking about the new iPod Matt has and all his other new stuff. How he's been out so much lately. How he skips track practices and comes up with weird excuses for getting home late. But he wouldn't have, would he? Surely not my brother.

Kat is standing beside me, wide-eyed. "Isn't it brutal," she says. "Who the heck did it, Maddy? That's what I want to know!"

"Me too," I say, as my gut begins to churn. I quicken my pace. It makes me sick to think about any of it anymore.

chapter nine

It's hard to concentrate during class. I can't help glancing at my classmates on the track team. It seems as if everyone who got lectured by Coach Reeves this morning is distracted. Who got ripped off? And who did it? And please don't let it be Matt!

Kids from the team that I pass in the hallways all have the same glum faces. When our eyes meet, we each know what the other is thinking. Our eyebrows raise in question. No one knows who to trust now.

How can a team function properly with *that* going on? It's like an ugly mark has been tattooed on all of us. And it's marred everything teamwork is supposed to stand for. I'm furious and worried at the same time. All sorts of nasty thoughts won't stop doing laps in my mind.

We're all solemn at practice after school. When something like this happens, you can't stop thinking somebody out there thinks *you* could be the guilty one. If you babble too much, it makes you look like you're covering up. If you're too quiet, it makes it look as if you're hiding something. But someone *is* hiding something!

No one leaves their backpacks in the change room, as we usually do. Not after what happened on Saturday. We line them up alongside the track, where they're in plain view.

I start running the track to get rid of the jitters I've had ever since Coach Reeves's nasty announcement this morning.

Kat, Paige and Isabel are out running already. They seem to be having some sort of serious conversation as they jog. No doubt it's about what happened, and I don't feel like talking about it with them.

Zenia runs on her own, lost in thought. Every once in a while, her eyes meet mine and she smiles weakly. I wish she would tell me what really happened on Saturday.

Shauna is running on the track too. It's as if she's trying to catch up with me instead of avoid me. I watch from the corner of my eye as she picks up speed, and I slow down a bit. But I refuse to say hi after she made me look like an idiot when I tried to wave at her the other day.

She's almost caught up to me, and her mouth is half open. Our eyes meet, lock for an instant. A shrill whistle sounds, and we all stop dead. Shauna blinks, turns around and runs with everyone else over to where Coach Reeves is standing next to the track.

"*Why so serious?*" Coach asks while we wait for our usual pep talk. He gives us an evil Joker grin. And that makes us all laugh nervously. We've seen the *Batman* movie he's quoting from. "Lots of stuff has to happen this week," he says. "Like making the relay team picks for the junior and senior grades. I'll let you know on Friday who'll be on each of the teams, including subs. Any questions?"

Silence.

"So you need to pump it up this week, sprinters. I need you to be totally focused. To give me your best times ever," Coach says. "And I want you to remember that even though this is a competition, you're competing to be part of a team. So I want to see smiles on your faces while you're totally busting your butts, okay?"

"Wow, *wicked*," a guy says. There's some snorts of laughter from some of the other guys.

Coach frowns. "Have you got a problem with that, Mr. Halstead?" he says. "And what about the rest of you guys that think Justin is so hilarious?"

I glance over at Shauna. She's frowning. Her eyes are burning into her brother's head like a sunbeam through a magnifying glass.

"I meant it in a good way, Coach Reeves," Justin murmurs, not glancing at anyone.

"Really?" Coach offers him a sly grin. "Still, fifty push-ups wouldn't hurt to convince me. Let's see them right now, Halstead. Feel free to join him, Carter, Braden, Noah. And anyone else who thinks this is funny."

Without another word, Justin is on the ground along with the two other guys who laughed. Carter is still grinning in his usual smug way.

"You too," Coach says, pointing at him.

Carter shrugs, drops into a handstand and walks a few steps.

Everyone laughs nervously except for Coach. "Make it one hundred, Carter," he says.

chapter ten

Everyone works extra hard at practice. Coach Reeves is on our cases. His face is stiff the entire time, and he keeps checking on Justin and Carter. He's not impressed.

Every time I stop to watch Matt, he's hurling a shot put. He's out to kill it, and I smile when I see Coach Chapman giving him a high five. I've never seen the sprinters run as fast as we are today. We know what's at stake this week. We all want to be part of the relay team. And the fastest one of us will get to run the 100-meter sprint.

Coach Reeves calls us to the starting line when it's our turn to race. We're last, of course, since ours is the bantam team. He always works his way down from the seniors. I feel young and green after watching the older kids compete.

As we line up, my blood races through my veins. Beside me, Kat is totally focused and stares straight ahead. Zenia seems more nervous than usual. She keeps glancing around. Coach glares at her. Shauna has a serious look on her face. She's tossed her hat onto the field. She means business.

When Coach yells, "Set," Zenia takes a step forward. Coach yells, "False start," and tells us to get back into position. False starts are a no-no. One too many, and you're in danger of disqualification. Zenia has never had a false start before.

And then she does it a second time. Then a third. Coach suggests maybe she should sit this one out because she doesn't seem focused. She shuffles over to her backpack, picks it up and heads toward the school doors. Poor Zenia! She's completely distracted. I can't imagine how humiliated she must feel right now.

Kat crosses the finish line only one step ahead of me. But it isn't even an issue this time. I'm worried about Zenia, and I think Kat is too. When a fellow teammate is having a hard time, it throws everyone off.

After practice, everybody scatters in different directions. I can't wait to get home, scarf down some of Abuelo's great cooking and call Zenia. When I reach for my backpack, I spot something crumpled stuck in the handle. It's a note.

"What's that?" Kat says. I spin around, and she's staring at the note in my hand.

I shrug. "Just a piece of trash, I guess." I shove it into the pocket of my shorts.

"God, what was up with Zenia today," Kat says. "Nothing was working for her."

"No clue. Can you wait a few minutes, Kat? I've got to grab some math homework from my locker."

"You actually like math, don't you, Maddy," Kat says with an easy smile. "That pretty much makes you a freak of nature, you know that, right?"

"Yep, and I'll be sure to remind you that you called me a *freak of nature* next time you need my help before a test," I say.

Kat laughs out loud, then hoists her backpack over her shoulder.

"Hope you don't mind if I take off," Kat says. "English essay due tomorrow. I haven't even started it yet."

"Okay, see ya later," I say as she jogs off. I'm dying to read the note that's practically sizzling in my pocket. As soon as she's out of sight, I quickly uncrumple it.

The note says, *Meet me after practice out back by the Dumpster*. I slip out the school's back doors and onto the field. The track is deserted, everyone is long gone. I'm uneasy as I head toward the Dumpster. When I turn the corner, Shauna is waiting for me.

Maybe she really was trying to talk to me earlier. But right now she looks too serious for this to be a white-flag-waving sort of conversation. I'm almost afraid to hear what she has to say.

chapter eleven

"Maddy, I need to talk to you about some-thing." The words race out of Shauna's mouth, and my heart skips a little when she says them.

"So what's up?" I ask, trying not to let on that she makes me nervous.

"It's about my brother," she says. "And yours, and what happened at practice Saturday."

My brother? *Gulp*.

"Okay," I say, trying to act cool.

"Well, Justin was fooling around with Carter and his crew..." She pauses and swallows hard. "What if Justin was in on it? What if *he* stole something too?" Her eyes narrow. "I hate that Justin and Carter are friends. Justin's totally going to blow his chances if he keeps messing up on the track."

"Wow, that sucks, Shauna." What a relief. At least she didn't tell me *my* brother was the thief.

"His lame attitude is throwing the whole boys' team off!" she says.

"Yeah, I've noticed," I say. "I mean, it's so obvious. And that whole push-up thing today. Coach Reeves was totally pissed."

"Coach threatened to kick Justin off the team if he doesn't get it together soon. If our parents find out he's screwing up, they'll lose it! Why does he need to show off so much?"

"Who knows? Maybe it's a guy thing, to prove how tough they are. Maybe it's to impress girls. Why are you telling me this, though, Shauna?" I ask her. "What can *I* do about it?"

"Well," she says, then pauses to stare down at her running shoes. "It's your brother, Matt. You know what *he's* like."

Uh-oh. Now she won't even look at me. "What about Matt?"

"Well, to start with, Justin thinks he's awesome. He has so much respect for him. Because of all the cool stuff he's into."

Wait, what? Did I hear wrong? Cool stuff he's into? What is she talking about? "Maybe you'd better fill me in, Shauna," I say. "Because at home right now, Matt is mostly a jerk."

Shauna's bright eyes open wide. "A jerk? How can a guy like him be a jerk? He's come over to my place to help me with science a couple of times. Last Saturday night, he dropped by for a while. He's on the track team *and* he's got a job. He's always so focused. And...you know...I kind of think he's good-looking too."

"Wait, *what*?" I'm not sure I heard her right again.

So she's crushing hard on my brother, a guy who helps her with schoolwork and also has a job? Most of what she's said doesn't make much sense to me. "What are you talking about? Maybe you have my brother mixed up with someone else."

Shauna laughs. "Don't think so," she says. "Trust me, Maddy. I know *exactly* who Matt Benez is."

I squint. "Okay, so then where exactly does he work?"

"Burger King. He's been there for a few months now. Haven't you ever been in to see him?"

Our family never eats at Burger King. *Ever*. Hmmm. Good place to work if you don't want your family to find out you have a job. But why wouldn't one of my friends tell me? And why wouldn't Matt?

"*Which* Burger King?" I say, growing more curious by the minute.

"It's across town," Shauna says. "I just happened to go there for lunch one day when I was shopping with my mom. He was behind the counter, wearing one of those goofy hats. That was when he offered to help me with science. Do you know if

57

he's going to the dance on Friday night?" She smiles coyly.

"No clue about the dance. Wow," I say.

I start to put the pieces of the puzzle together. Late nights, out often, new stuff all the time—apparently my brother has a job. He might even have a girlfriend, who he's helping with science. And my family's been in the dark about it all.

"Why are you telling me all this, Shauna?" I ask, still confused.

"Because I need your help, Maddy," she says. "I need you and Matt to help me help my brother get his act together before it's too late."

"Before it's too late? Really? You do realize Justin could outrun the Roadrunner!"

I try to laugh, hoping to coax another smile out of Shauna. But her face is still bleak.

"You must have noticed he sucks on the track these days, Maddy," she says. "He isn't focused. And he acts like a goof all the time. My parents are so proud of him, especially since some American colleges started scouting him. It will kill them if he screws up and blows his chance at a scholarship." She sighs. "I wish I could be *half* as good as he is!"

"Yeah, I know the feeling. My brother is a natural too." I shrug and shake my head. "I sure wish I could figure out why Matt hasn't told Mom and Abuelo what he's up to. Why does it have to be such a big secret?"

"I'm sure he has his reasons," Shauna says. "And I'm sure my brother does too. If only we could figure out what they are."

Shauna frowns, then kicks a rock and watches it bounce off the Dumpster. I stand in silence. I realize I've misjudged Shauna. Now is the perfect time to ask her my burning question once and for all.

chapter twelve

I take a deep breath, and when Shauna looks up, I lock my eyes on hers. "Shauna, I'm going to be totally honest with you. Sometimes it seems as if you can't stand me or anyone else on the team."

Finally a half smile blooms on Shauna's face. "Well, the truth is, it really bugs me that you and Kat keep on beating me, you know. I guess I've been taking my frustration out on everyone."

"Seriously?" I open my eyes wide, and she laughs.

"Seriously. But I'm trying to get past it. I'm really competitive. I hate losing. Plus, I'm stressed about my brother and kind of watching out for him."

Now it's all starting to make sense. "But you'll *still* be on the relay team," I say. "Even if you're not the hundred-meter runner."

"That's not good enough, Maddy," she says, folding her arms and staring off into the distance. "So do you think you and Matt can help my brother, or what?"

"Okay, I'll try and figure something out with Matt," I say. "Listen. Why don't you come sit with me at lunch in the caf some time? It would be a great way for you to get to know some of the girls on our team better."

"Hmmm, maybe," Shauna says. "I'll think about it, Maddy."

By the time Shauna and I say goodbye, I've promised to do what I can to help her out with her brother.

I feel sorry for Shauna. I know what it's like to want to win so bad and then not have it happen. No wonder she's always cross at track practice. Besides competing with Kat and me on the track, she's also competing with her brother's success. She's jealous of him, yet she wants him to succeed. Knowing all this makes me feel closer to her.

I like having a new friend who confides in me. I'm half tempted to call and talk to Kat about it, since she's my best friend. But how would that help? If she knows how much Shauna wants to win, it could make her work even harder. And I want to win too! Maybe it's better to keep my mouth shut.

I grab my math homework from my locker and hurry home. I can't wait to see Matt and ask him about his job and his maybe girlfriend. When I burst through the door, I can smell dinner cooking. I head straight for the stove, peck Abuelo on the cheek and peek at what's in the pot he's stirring.

"Is that cheese sauce?" I ask. "And is that macaroni cooking? Are you seriously making macaroni and cheese, Abuelo?"

My grandfather grins sheepishly and nods. "I found a recipe on that goggle thing you showed me how to use," he says.

"You mean Google? You actually googled a recipe! You're amazing, Abuelo. How come?" My grandfather has never made mac and cheese, I'm sure. He doesn't even like us to buy KD. He says it's too gluey. And here he is, making his own version.

"Well, you know," he says and shrugs, "Mateo, he wants me to try something new. So now I'm trying something new. Hope he likes it."

"If it tastes as good as it smells, it's sure to be great," I say. "Is Matt home yet?"

"In his room. He says for me to cook fast. He has to go out. Again. Where's he going all the time anyway? With those baggy pants of his." He shakes his head and starts stirring again.

"I keep telling you, Abuelo. Don't worry about it, okay?" I feel a whole lot better saying that now that I'm starting to believe it myself.

I hustle down the hallway and knock on Matt's door.

"What's up?" he says, without opening it.

"I need to talk to you," I say.

"Can't right now. I'm kind of busy," Matt says. So I knock again. "What is your problem? I'm trying to get an assignment done. Quit bugging me."

"Why can't you do it tonight?" I ask.

"Because I have to be somewhere! What's *with* you today?"

I pause. Smile at the sweet rush I'm about to get.

"Where do you have to be, Matt? Your Burger King job, or Shauna's place?" The words are like candy in my mouth.

Matt's door swings slowly open. He stares at me as if I've just announced the world is about to end.

chapter thirteen

"Shh!" Matt pulls me into his room and shuts the door. "How did you find out, Maddy?"

"Oh, I have my sources," I say and sit on his bed.

"Who ratted me out? Oh. Wait. Shauna, right?" When I nod, he sighs and sinks onto the bed beside me. "She didn't know that I hadn't told you guys about my job."

"No kidding. I was totally shocked when she told me. So where do you stash your uniform anyway?"

"I just leave it at work. Someone takes it home and washes it for me. They're really nice and understanding there." He shrugs and sighs. "So are you going to blab it to Mom and Abuelo, or what?"

"Blab? I don't get it, Matt. Why don't you just tell them yourself? Why don't you want them to find out? What's the big secret?"

"Got any more questions?" He raises his eyebrows at me. "Don't you get how complicated this is, Maddy? You know what Abuelo is like, how proud he is. He hates to feel that we're taking care of him, so he tries to take care of us."

"Yeah, so why would it matter if you have a job?"

Matt sighs again and scrubs his fingers through his thick dark hair. "Because I don't want Mom and Abuelo to think I need more than they can give me. Don't you see? I like having stuff. Like the iPod I bought off Craigslist. I don't want to bother them for money I know they probably don't have. I want to pay for stuff myself. I also don't want them to worry that I might be sacrificing my schoolwork because of a job. You get it *now*?"

Oh yeah, I get it all right. *Finally.* "So is that why you missed track practice on Friday? And why you've been keeping such weird hours all the time?"

Matt nods slowly. "I can't pick and choose all my shifts. Sometimes I have to work lousy ones. They know I have school *and* track, and they try to do the best they can with that. Sometimes I have to cover for people. Like last Friday, I worked two shifts and booked it home on my bike in between. It's tough squeezing everything in. But I'm saving for a car. Might actually be able to buy one in a couple of years. Something I can fix up. God, I did *so not* want to have this conversation."

He stops babbling and looks straight into my eyes. I reach out and give him a quick hug.

"You rock, Mateo," I say, and he smiles.

I ask him about Shauna and find out he likes her, but he says he can't really give her much of his time. So they're just friends for now. He says that could change. He never told us when he was going over to Shauna and Justin's place because he doesn't want Abuelo to know about him having a sort-of girlfriend. It would only make him worry about Matt losing focus at school and track. And if Mom found out, she'd never be able to *not* tell Abuelo. She blabs absolutely everything to our grandfather.

"How well do you know Justin Halstead anyway, Matt?" I ask. "You guys are friends, aren't you? In some of the same classes?"

"We talk sometimes, train together, but that's about it. He seems okay. Acts kind of goofy and shows off a bit. Just like Carter and some of those other guys. Which the coaches aren't digging so much. Amazing athlete though. I'm pretty sure Shauna's worried about him. For a lot of reasons."

"Major worried, Matt. And Shauna told me Justin looks up to you."

Matt's eyebrows shoot up. "Why would he look up to me? He's the better athlete."

"Maybe he's a better runner, but absolutely everyone watches when you throw that shot put, for some crazy reason," I say with an eye roll and then laugh when he blushes.

"I'm glad you know what's going on," Matt says with a sheepish grin. "It was hard to keep it a secret for three months. So what else did Shauna say?"

"She can't figure out why Justin's been acting like such a jerk lately. He has so much potential. He's actually getting scouted already," I say.

Matt shakes his head. "I know. If I were him, I'd be totally focused on the track. But he likes to make people laugh. A class-clown dude. And it feeds right into Carter's lame attitude. That doesn't work for Coach Reeves. You can tell he's getting fed up."

"I can't believe Carter can't get his act together," I say. "Shauna asked me if we can help her with Justin. See if we can keep him out of trouble, get him to focus. How do we do that?"

"We'll figure something out," he says and pats me on the head like I'm a little kid or something. I playfully swat his hand away.

"Mateo! Madina! Dinner!" Abuelo's voice down the hall makes us jump to our feet.

"Can't wait to try that mac and cheese," Matt says. He stops me at the door. "You won't tell Mom, right, Maddy? Promise?"

I nod and smile.

A few seconds later, we're sitting at the table scarfing down macaroni and cheese. Abuelo couldn't resist adding his Spanish touch to it by throwing in some fried chorizo sausage. It's awesome.

Abuelo has an ear-to-ear grin. "You like my North American cooking, Mateo?" he says.

Matt nods, his mouth too stuffed to answer.

Mom comes in the door a few minutes later and sits down to eat with us. It's the first time in ages we've all eaten together. Mom chats away with Matt like she always does whenever he sticks around long enough.

I admire her for what she said on Saturday. She's right. Sometimes you have to let your guard down and trust people and hope they'll do the right thing. That's easy enough at home, but I sure wish

I could feel the same way about trusting the kids on my track team. *Friends gather no dust*, Jesse Owens said. But after the theft, I don't know what to think anymore.

I'm so relieved to know the truth about Matt's activities, I concentrate on getting every last drop of cheese sauce off my plate. I try not to think about the call I have to make after dinner.

I dial Zenia's number after the kitchen is cleaned up. And, yet again, all she gives me are excuses. She says a calf cramp caused the false starts today. I'm not convinced. Clearly whatever happened on Saturday is playing on her mind and affecting her on the track.

And when it affects her, it affects the rest of us too.

chapter fourteen

Tuesday morning practice goes well for a change, for most of us. Coach Reeves doesn't start off with a lecture. Only his usual words of encouragement and reminders about doing our best. Because his decisions are waiting to be made.

Only one person is getting flak from Coach Reeves, and that's Justin. He shows up a few minutes late and has to do push-ups because of it. He goofs off the whole time he's doing them and makes the other guys laugh. Which is not amusing for Coach. Shauna rolls her eyes and shakes her head when she sees her brother acting stupid again.

When it's time to get serious, he doesn't run well at all. Coach starts lecturing and accuses Justin of not being focused. He may be a rocket in the 100 and 400 meter, but the way it's going right now, he might not even make the relay team. He's that close to getting dumped. Whenever Coach raises his voice to blast Justin, I can't help notice Shauna cringe. She's trying to look out for her brother, but he just keeps blowing it. If only Matt and I could come up with a decent plan to help.

This morning, Zenia is quiet. She's focused on her racing and doesn't say much to the rest of us. I catch her watching some of the guys from time to time and realize a few of them are also watching her. Especially Carter.

At one point, I actually catch them in an exchange. When Zenia glances in his direction, I spot him press a finger up against his lips. His eyes lock on hers. I can guess what he's telling her when Zenia quickly turns away. *Keep your mouth shut*. No wonder Zenia has been so quiet the last couple of days. No wonder she made those false starts. She's scared. She knows too much.

In the change room after practice, I try to talk to her. She's alone on a bench changing out of her runners.

"You were amazing today in the high jump," I say. "And on the track. I can't believe how close we all are, you, me, Shauna and Kat."

Zenia smirks. "Yeah, but you guys are always one step ahead, aren't you."

"It's weird, isn't it?" I say. "If Kat wins one race, I win the next one. We end up breaking even all the time. There's no escaping it. And it's driving Coach Reeves crazy!"

"It's pretty much guaranteed that we'll all be on the same relay team," Zenia says as she goes back to changing her shoes.

"You know, I saw what Carter did out there," I say, knowing nobody else can hear us over the girls' chatter echoing off the concrete walls.

Zenia narrows her eyes. "What are you talking about, Maddy?"

"He was telling you to keep quiet. I *saw* him, Zenia. What does he want you to keep quiet about anyway?" Is she going to give it up now, or will I have to tell her what I saw on Saturday? I really don't want to.

Her mouth is a tight line. "Don't worry about it, okay?" she says. "He...he was just goofing around, that's all."

"Is that why you made all those false starts yesterday, Zenia? Was he giving you grief then too? If you know something, you should say something, don't you think?"

Her eyes stray sideways. "Why do you keep bugging me about it?" she says. "Why do you think I know something?"

I shrug. I can't confess what I saw on Saturday. I can't admit I did nothing to help her. So I let it go, and I let her go. I watch as she saunters out of the change room and leaves me sitting with all my questions still unanswered.

At lunchtime in the caf on Tuesday, a group of the old Wentworth gang gathers around a table to chow down and have some laughs.

I spot Shauna, with her lunch, headed for our table. I keep thinking maybe she'll swerve off to another table, but no. She plops into the empty chair beside me, says hi, and opens her lunch bag. Kat and Zenia look completely baffled. Nobody is saying much. It's as if they're not sure about Shauna and are upset she had the guts to sit with us, which is something that bugs me about high school. Some of my old middle-school friends are afraid to make new friends. I was, too, until I got to know Shauna a bit better. I'm glad she's decided to suck it up and sit with us today.

"Hey," I say, "how's it going? You were burning up the track this morning."

"Thanks. Just trying to do my best." She smiles, then looks at my friends. They're staring at her as if an alien landed at our table instead of a classmate.

Kat narrows her eyes. Nobody says anything. So it's up to me to make conversation. I start to babble about anything and everything. I keep checking the clock, hoping lunchtime will end soon. But I don't need to worry long, because within a few minutes everyone has wandered off, including Kat and Zenia.

"Wow, that went well," Shauna says.

I shrug. "It was good you took a chance. Maybe it'll be easier next time."

In middle school, friendships were so much easier.

chapter fifteen

After school on Tuesday, everything changes. I know from the moment our coaches show up on the track that we're about to hear some more lousy news. When Coach Reeves blows his whistle, we all hustle over. I wish I could make a run for it so I won't have to hear what's coming next.

"Well, boys and girls," he says in a low voice. "I think we may have had a break in Saturday's theft. Someone came forward and told us what they saw. So you'll notice a face missing on the team."

Everyone starts to look around. Who is missing?

"And right now," Coach Chapman says, "he's in the office, having a meeting with the principal and vice-principals to decide if he should be suspended from school for the rest of the week. They're trying to get the whole story out of him."

I have a brief flash of hope. Maybe Zenia finally said something! Maybe the truth about what I saw, about what I know, never has to come out. My teammates are still turning their heads in every direction to try and figure out who's missing.

Coach Reeves holds up one hand. "Look. The rest of you have to carry on. It isn't your problem. Focus on your events, on being the best that you can be on the track and on the field. That's your job right now. Not yapping among yourselves about what happened."

Everyone nods. Our coaches are depending on us to perform at our best no matter what. But it's going to be hard.

Especially for Shauna, whose face is sagging. It's Justin who's missing today. Matt glances at me and shakes his head. We've let Shauna down. I only hope it isn't too late for Justin Halstead. I wonder who turned him in.

And then I hear someone say something and turn around.

"Major bummer. It sure sucks to be Justin right now, doesn't it?" Carter says. He has a strange smirk on his face. One of relief, maybe even triumph, like he just won a race or something. But I can tell Zenia is completely shocked. She stares at Carter with disgust. Then she shakes her head and stalks toward the school doors.

I run after her. I can't help it. I just have to know. "What's going on?" I say. "Where are you going?"

"To see the principal," she says, shaking her mane of hair in fury. "Something is wrong. It wasn't only Justin hanging around those bags on Saturday. Carter was there too, and some other guys. There's no proof who actually *did* do it, and Justin is getting blamed. Carter knows I saw something going on though. He saw me watching him, and when I tried to confront him about it, he started shoving me around."

"So you saw those guys messing with the backpacks and tried to ask them about it? God, Zenia, you've got guts!"

"Not only that," she adds. "I didn't know it at the time, but it was *my* smartphone that got ripped off! There were lots of kids hanging around the backpacks that day. So it's hard to say exactly *who* did it. But Justin isn't the one."

She has a funny smile on her face. Is she crushing on Justin?

"Oh god, Zenia. So *that's* what happened on Saturday. That's why Carter and his friends were giving you a hard time after everyone left." *Crap.* I cover my mouth.

Zenia stops dead. "What did you just say?" she asks in a low voice. "You mean you were *there*? You saw what happened?"

I nod slowly. "I was way over by the school though. I couldn't even see who it was. And I was scared, Zenia. I was a total chicken, and I'm so sorry."

"You think I wasn't scared too? You didn't even try to do something to *help* me. I can't believe it." She spins around and marches into the school.

What a complete and total jerk I am. How will I ever make it up to Zenia? How will I even be able to face her again? What kind of a team will we be if we keep getting sidetracked with all these problems?

I shuffle back to join the rest of the team. I feel as if I'm wearing lead runners. Everyone is watching me. I'm sure they're wondering what Zenia and I were talking about. Coach Reeves has an eye on me too. He raises his eyebrows, and I just shrug. When he launches into his usual pep talk, I can barely hear what he's saying, I'm so rattled.

The coach winds up and sends us off to do our warm-ups. As I'm about to head for the track, fingers grip my arm and dig in hard.

"Hey!" I yank myself loose and spin around.

Carter is standing there grinning and frowning at the same time. "How's it going, Maddy?" he says.

"It's going fine, Carter." I try to edge away from him. Just having him this close to me is making me sweat.

"What was Zenia whining about? What's her problem? Is something wrong?"

I'm close to tears. What's become of this guy I thought I knew last year? I even went to an eighth-grade grad barbecue at his place with the whole track team. Was that only a year ago? What is he trying to prove?

"Of course something's wrong, Carter. Everything's wrong. Don't you get it? Coach Reeves is freaking out. The team is sucking. And there's only one person who can fix things."

Carter narrows his eyes and pushes his face close to mine. "Stay out of it, Maddy. It's none of your business."

He lopes over to the track and starts running. I watch the back of him, wondering how we'll ever get this team to pull together with so much tension in the air.

We carry on as best we can with Justin and Zenia missing from practice. Everyone's wondering what's going on in

the principal's office. And Coach Reeves
seems uneasy. He dismisses us before they
come back. Kat is icy for the entire practice, and then she takes off without even
saying goodbye. Matt and I wait around
with Shauna for a while, but when Justin
and Zenia don't come out, we give up and
walk home.

chapter sixteen

I find out what really happened from Shauna when she phones me later that evening. Zenia's report to the principal changed everything. They had to let Justin go because they don't know *who* is telling the truth. Justin is keeping his mouth shut. He won't tell Shauna anything. It's as if he's covering for Carter or afraid to speak up.

Shauna can't figure out why a guy like Carter, who is younger than her brother, has such an effect on him. I tell her people get a kick out of Carter because they think he's cool. And this year he has a bigger audience. He looks and acts way older than he actually is. Girls want him, and guys want to be him, so now his head is too big for the rest of his body. I reassure Shauna that at least Justin has another chance now. At least he didn't get suspended.

By the time I hang up, my thoughts are spinning. Who ratted out Justin in the first place? I hope it isn't who I think it is. How will I ever gain back Zenia's trust and friendship? Why is Kat acting so weird now? Who is Coach going to choose to run the 100 meter? If it's Kat, will I be able to handle it? And if it's me, will she?

I manage to get to sleep in spite of all my racing thoughts. The early-morning sun lights up my room when I open my eyes on Wednesday. Something feels different. For probably the first time, I'm not looking forward to practice this morning. I have to face Zenia, Kat, Shauna and all our problems. I dread being on the track with them.

Luckily we don't have to compete against one another this morning. All we do is our plyometrics and warm-up sprints. None of us has much to say, either, but I can almost hear what they're thinking. Everyone notices our silence. Coach Reeves has an eye on us. He can see his potential relay team has some issues.

When he calls me over, my legs go weak. I hope he isn't going to ask about Justin and Carter. Did Zenia tell him what I saw and that I never helped her?

"I'm not asking you girls to race today. I'm holding off. Is there something you need to tell me, Maddy?" Our coach is obviously worried about us. There's a softness in his voice that I've never heard before.

Should I confide in Coach Reeves? No, I can't tell him anything yet. I need more time to sort things out myself.

"Not really, Coach," I say. "I think everyone is a bit uptight over what's been going on this week. We're all worried about our teammates."

"Maybe so," he says. "But remember, I'm here if you need me."

"I'll keep that in mind." I offer him a weak smile, hoping it doesn't reveal how much I'm holding inside.

If this keeps up, some of the other sprinters may move up into our positions. And the rest of us will be left behind, wondering what just happened to our relay team.

Coach Reeves doesn't race us at afternoon practice on Wednesday either. He knows something nasty is going on. It's as if he doesn't want to make us compete when there is so much upset right now. Instead, he makes us run endlessly around the track and hop madly up and down. It's a great distraction and burns off a lot of excess energy and worries. Matt has his eye on me. He knows something is going on with me and my friends.

It's obvious from our silence. Every time our eyes meet, he raises his eyebrows.

Justin seems to be behaving today. Shauna shoots him invisible arrows, warning him about something. Carter is his usual arrogant self, running his butt off. When Coach isn't watching, he fools around with some of the other guys. If only something or someone could bring Carter down a few notches. If *only*!

After practice I walk home with Kat, Paige and Isabel. Zenia is long gone, and so is Shauna. As soon as Coach let us go, they didn't stick around. They took off in opposite directions as if they had somewhere important to be. Shauna was right behind Justin when he left. She seems to be sticking to him like stink on a skunk to watch his every move and keep him in line.

Zenia totally ignored me today. I'm getting bad vibes from her. But I don't blame her. Problem is, I'm getting some bad vibes from my other friends now too. I'm sure it's about what happened in the caf when Shauna sat with us. Everyone thinks my BFF loyalties are changing. Kat will always be my first and best friend. But now that I've gotten to know Shauna and understand her a bit better, I want to be friends with her too.

I'm quiet as we walk home. Kat, Paige and Isabel babble away about the dance coming up on Friday night. They talk about what they're going to wear and who they want to dance with. Every time I look up, one of them is staring at me.

Finally Paige asks, "What is *going on* with you? And what's with Shauna. I can't believe she sat at our table in the caf yesterday. At least she didn't try it again today."

"I thought you didn't even like Shauna because she's always giving everyone the evil eye on the track," Isabel adds. "That's what Kat said anyway."

I stop walking and stare at them, three of my oldest friends. "I never said I didn't *like* her. I just wondered why she didn't like us. And now I know what her problem is, so it's not a big deal anymore. Shauna and I got it all straightened out."

"But Kat is still your best friend, right?" Paige asks. "And not Shauna. So why are you being nice to her when she's acting like such a loser?"

"What are you talking about?" I glare at them in disbelief. "Shauna is on our *team*! Don't you think being friends with her is a *good* thing? We've hardly gotten to know any of the other kids at school this year. We're always stuck together like some dumb snotty clique."

"*What*?" Paige and Isabel say and gasp.

"Just let it go, you guys," Kat says. "If that's what you really think of us, Maddy, then *whatever*."

"Whatever is *right*." I shake my head. I can't believe they're not even interested enough to ask what Shauna and I straightened out. I'm so furious, I make a run for it without looking back.

chapter seventeen

By the time I get home, I'm almost in tears. I already regret blurting out such awful things instead of trying to explain to my friends that Matt and I are trying to figure out how to help Shauna. I flop down on my bed and bury my face in a novel for English class until I get called for dinner.

Abuelo has cooked up a *paella* tonight. I know Matt won't complain. It's one of his favorites. He would even choose it over mac and cheese.

At dinner, Matt and I keep glancing at each other. We still haven't had a chance to talk about what went on at practice today. Mom doesn't seem overly concerned, even though I'm sure she notices. Abuelo always takes his cue from Mom. The two of them chat away together, completely ignoring our signals.

Mom trusts us. I know that now. She doesn't feel the need to snoop, to try to pry stuff out of us. I've heard other kids call their parents "crowbars" because of all the prying into their lives that they do. Some even creep their kids' Facebook pages to spy.

Awhile later, when Mom and Abuelo are relaxing in the living room and we're cleaning up the kitchen, we finally have a chance to talk.

"Did you see Shauna today?" Matt asks in a low voice. "She was all over Justin. Watching him all the time. Glaring whenever he goofed off."

"I saw that. We've gotta come up with a way to help," I say. "We promised Shauna we would. The coaches are just waiting for

93

a chance to make an example of someone so they can whip the team into shape."

"Zenia was watching Justin too," Matt says, grinning. "But for totally different reasons. I've heard about those two. Everyone notices the way they stare at each other."

"Yeah, I know. It's hard to miss," I say.

"What's up with you, Zenia and Kat? Usually the three of you run laps together and never stop talking. You guys ignored each other today. Don't deny it. And what was Coach talking with you about? Why didn't he race you the way he always does?"

I blink, not sure what to say. Was it so obvious that even Matt noticed?

"Oh, it's no big deal, Matt," I say. "Coach still isn't sure who'll be running the hundred meter. So he's holding off on racing us. He'll be making the big decision soon though."

I feel a sharp little stab of guilt for not coming clean with my brother about what I saw, especially after he finally came clean with me. And I'm trying my best not to fixate on what happened with Zenia or between Kat, Paige, Isabel and me. But it's very hard.

When my cell phone rings, I grab it and look at the name on the display, hoping it's Kat. But no. "It's Shauna," I say to Matt. "Hello?"

Shauna starts talking right away. "Maddy. This is getting worse. I just listened in on a phone call to my brother. I was outside his room when I heard his cell phone ring."

"Hang on!" I repeat all this to Matt and he leans in to hear. "Okay, go on, Shauna."

She tells us she heard her brother talking about the dance Friday night. They plan on partying before and after. She's sure she heard Justin say Carter's name.

"I'm scared they have something dumb planned for Friday," Shauna says. "I'm worried they'll do something stupid and get suspended or maybe even expelled. I don't want Justin to be a part of this anymore. He has too much to lose, maybe even a college track scholarship!"

Matt shakes his head and frowns. "Did you try talking to him?" he asks.

"Matt? Is that you?" Shauna's voice softens. She is *so* into my brother. "Yeah,

I tried, but he totally dissed me. Told me to quit my stupid worrying and that I'm not his mother, but I can't help it. Okay, I gotta go. He's coming now. We need to think of something fast!"

The line goes dead. Matt and I stare at my phone.

"Come on, *think*, Matt! Justin can't mess up his chances on the team *or* at school!"

Matt shrugs. "I have to work on Friday night," he says. "I can't even be at the dance to try and keep Justin from hanging out with those dudes. Maybe someone else could help us?"

A lightbulb goes on in my head. I *know* who could.

"Zenia. She likes him. And he likes her," I say.

My brother's face brightens. "Perfect. Do you think she'd help us out?"

I gulp. It isn't going to be easy. I don't even know if she'll talk to me right now. But I can't tell Matt that.

"Um..." I hesitate. "Okay, I'll see what I can do."

Matt offers me a high five. I take it and hope I won't let a whole bunch of people down.

chapter eighteen

By Thursday, I can't focus on the track or in the classroom. How can I ask Zenia for her help? I don't even know how to approach her.

Coach still doesn't race us on Thursday. He has us try to improve our times individually. He won't tell us our times either. He's holding off on making his decision for as long as he can. He explains to me that he wants to wait until Monday now. He asks if the situation is any closer to getting straightened out. I nod quickly, even though it isn't true.

Kat has been acting different ever since our blowup yesterday. I know I might have made a mistake saying what I did, but it just came out. Now it's as if our friendship is dissolving right before my eyes! She hangs out with Zenia while I run laps beside Shauna. It's as if she's making a point of letting me know that if I've found another BFF, so has she. It's like me and Shauna against Kat and Zenia.

What kind of relay team will that make? It's crazy! And what's so bad about having new friends anyway? Something is going to have to change if we ever hope to pull our relay team together. We have to find a way to trust each other again. At least I have Shauna to walk home with today. We're still trying to find a way to keep Justin out of trouble Friday night.

After dinner, I go to my room to study for a social studies test. Matt raps on my door and peers in.

"So what did Zenia say, Maddy? Will she help us with Justin?"

"Well…" I sigh. "I actually haven't asked her yet, Matt."

Finally I tell him what happened to Zenia last Saturday, and how I blew it as a friend. He sinks down on my bed and puts his head in his hands. He has trouble looking at me. I can't blame him. I can hardly look at myself in the mirror these days.

"I'm not surprised about Carter. *At all*," says Matt. But don't…" He pauses. "Don't you think you're still being a chicken by not trying to do something about it now? By not trying to talk to Zenia, at least?"

I swallow loudly. He's right.

"Someone's got to make the first move," he says.

"Okay." I slap my hands on my knees. "I'll do it. Right now."

"I *knew* you'd do the right thing, Maddy," he says and smiles.

Which gives me the last little nudge I need to pick up my phone. I go out and sit on the front steps. I punch in Zenia's cell number, and she answers right away.

"Zenia. We need your help with something," I say. I explain how we need her help with Justin and that he might be headed for trouble with Carter and the other guys on Friday night.

But she cuts me off. "Hold on. What does any of this have to do with me?"

"Well, you know, you stopped him from getting suspended. We...we kind of thought maybe you cared about him, maybe more than just as a friend. If you could try to sidetrack him at the dance on Friday night... so he stays away from Carter and the other jerks. So he stays out of trouble..." My voice dwindles away.

There. I got it out. It's done. I tried. There's a long pause. I'm starting to think she's going to hang up.

"Zenia," I say, "I still feel awful about what happened on Saturday at the track..."

"Maddy, it's nobody's business what's going on between me and Justin,"

Zenia murmurs. "And how can you call me after what you did? Anyway, I'm not even going to the dance. Bye."

And she hangs up. I have absolutely no idea what to do next.

Matt is in the doorway. "What did she say?" he asks hopefully.

I sigh. I can't turn around to look at him. "She said she'd think about it."

chapter nineteen

Everything is falling apart, and it's my fault. Most of my friends aren't talking to me. I have to try and fix things, at least with Kat. I have to explain why I said what I did. After Matt disappears into the house, I take a deep breath and dial Kat's number. She answers on the first ring.

"What's up?" she says. Not even hello. Not a good start.

"Kat, I know you're still mad at me," I say.

"Can you at least let me try to explain what I meant yesterday?"

"I'm pretty sure I know what you meant. But go ahead, Maddy," she says. There's an awkward pause. I don't know where to begin.

"Look, we have to find a way to pull this team together for everyone's sake. For yours, for Zenia's, and even for Shauna's. We have to find a way to trust each other and work together, or it won't be good."

"That doesn't change what you said to me, and to Isabel and Paige too. That was a lousy thing to say. I can't believe you really feel that way."

Kat's words bite because they're true.

"All I was trying to say is that we need to get to know other kids too. I didn't mean for it to come out the way it did. Don't you make mistakes sometimes?"

"Yeah, I do," Kat says. "And my biggest one is letting you beat me on the track—just for the sake of our...friendship."

I gasp. I can't help it. I can't believe what I'm hearing. She's actually been letting me win races!

"Kat. Why? Why would you do that?" I ask.

"I was faster than you last year, right? I think it bugged you, even though you said it didn't. Am I right?" Dead silence. She's waiting for my answer, but I can't speak. "Well? Am I right, Maddy?"

She is. Kat's totally right. I never admitted it. I just sucked up the losses, the way I thought a good friend should. Good friends leave their competitiveness on the track. That's what our coach told us last year. I murmur "Uh-huh" into my phone.

"Okay, so don't get mad when I tell you this." Her voice sounds thick with emotion. "This year I wanted you to believe you were as good as me for the sake of our friendship. I wanted Coach Reeves to make the decision about who was faster. But the truth is, you *still* can't beat me, Maddy. So that's it. Now I'm in it to win it."

I am stunned. "*Seriously*? You've been letting me win all along?"

"That's right," Kat says. "But not anymore."

I hang up because there's nothing more to say. I don't understand why she's been doing this. Maybe I never will.

Friday is a blur. I can barely focus. I still can't get over what Kat admitted last night. I'm sure I blow my social studies test. The coaches cancel practice and tell us to do some work on our own. They know that most of the team is pumped for the dance and not focused enough. I'm sure they're fed up with all the drama. And then there's the dance to deal with tonight. Coach Reeves is chaperoning. He'll be there, watching us all.

I can hardly face anyone. Not Shauna, or Zenia and Kat, who are both still giving me the cold shoulder. I don't even want to go near the dance tonight, but I know I have to. I promised Shauna I'd help her with Justin.

Butterflies race around in my gut all day. I can barely eat Abuelo's dinner, let alone look at him. He knows something is up, and so does Mom, but they won't ask.

Nobody says a word when Matt takes off after he inhales his dinner. He starts work at six on Friday nights.

After dinner, I pick out something cool to wear to the dumb dance even though I couldn't care less about it. I'd much rather be going for a run instead. I choose a denim skirt, a lime-green Old Navy T-shirt, and sandals because it's a warm night. I slap on a bit of makeup, not even caring how it looks, and head for the door.

I've never been crazy about dances. I hate standing there hoping someone will ask me to dance. Or worse—dancing in a circle with a bunch of other girls who nervously show off because nobody has asked them to dance. The competition at a school dance is more intense than at a race!

Before the dance, kids hang around outside the school. They gather in groups to check each other out. Some of them have a buzz on, as usual. Some others like me don't even want to be here. But no one wants to feel like a loser and stay home to hang out in cyberspace while their friends are here.

All my so-called friends are here. Kat's standing with Paige and Isabel. When our eyes meet, I look the other way. I still can't believe that she's been letting me win races. It makes me cringe just to think about it. A bunch of our other track friends are in the gym too. Carter isn't with them. He's hanging with his new crew instead. Justin and a bunch of other guys are already acting like jerks.

Some of the girls nearby are impressed by them. I'm not. Neither is Shauna, judging from her pissed-off face. She's standing by the doors, waiting for me as planned. We're going to keep an eye on things, try to sidetrack Justin if we can. Try to stop any trouble from finding him tonight. I don't want to pay the ten bucks and get my hand stamped. But I do, and I walk into the gym.

It's filled with blasting speakers, loud kids, hot stinky air and teachers who wish they were anywhere else but here. What a waste of half of my weekly allowance.

chapter twenty

Shauna and I are on the alert. Even when we're dancing, we're keeping one eye on Justin. I dance with Nathaniel and Zack, and a couple of guys I've met this year.

As the evening progresses, Justin and his friends start acting like goofs. It's almost as if they want to get told to leave. The teachers don't seem too thrilled with their fooling around, stupid dance moves, loud yelps and knocking into people. They seem to be trying to turn the gym into a mosh pit.

Coach Reeves's face is like a stone. A teacher taps Carter on the shoulder and says something to him. Carter nods solemnly and turns back to his friends, grinning and laughing. Every time I glance at Shauna, she's watching Justin and cringing.

At around 9:30, my cell phone vibrates. I whip the phone out of my pocket. It's a text from Zenia. It says, *Changed my mind...on my way now.* I almost want to do wind sprints around the gym!

"She's coming," I say to Shauna. But Shauna has no idea what I'm talking about. She frowns and looks at me, perplexed. "Just hang in there," I say.

A few minutes later, Zenia walks through the gym doors. She looks amazing! She has on a funky pink dress that practically lights up the room. Justin's head turns in her direction. His eyes lock on hers. This plan might actually work! Shauna sees what's going on, too, and smiles.

Zenia works her way through the maze of dancers and walks up to me. "Thanks for trying to help Justin," she says. "And for asking me to help. You're a good friend, Maddy. Even if you are a bit of a chicken sometimes."

"*Huh!*" I gasp, and Zenia starts laughing.

"Honestly, you rock, Maddy." She gives my arm a quick squeeze. Then she pushes her way through the crowd, walks over to Justin and asks him to dance.

Shauna and I watch as Justin and Zenia move closer and closer together even though it's not a slow dance. Clearly their romance has been waiting to break wide open. There's a quick kiss from Justin, and Shauna elbows me in the ribs. We're both grinning madly. The other jackass guys are dancing together, making a scene and being way too noisy. The teachers are gathered together, whispering among themselves and making plans. I can't watch anymore. So I hook my arm through Shauna's and drag her out into the hallway.

"It's awesome," I say. "He's totally distracted by her!"

Shauna nods. "You planned this whole thing, didn't you? You're brilliant, Maddy!"

"It was Matt's idea too," I say. "He couldn't be here. But we asked Zenia for help. And she came through!"

Someone stalks out the gym doors. It's Coach Reeves. He has a scary look on his face, like a thunderstorm about strike. Right behind him is Carter, and some of the other guys. They're surrounded by the teacher chaperones, who herd them out of the gym, down the hall and toward the school exit.

"Please tell me my brother *isn't* with them." Shauna's voice is hoarse.

"Hang on," I say, grabbing her arm. "Let's take a closer look."

He's not there. Justin *isn't* one of the guys being escorted out of the school tonight. Our plan actually worked! Shauna's mouth splits into a wide smile.

The teachers wander back into the gym after kicking out the troublemakers. Everyone seems relieved. Especially Coach Reeves. He walks over and looks us right in the eye.

"Carter was the one who told me he saw Justin hanging around the backpacks last Saturday." Coach sighs and shakes his head. "But I was never sold on his story. It's a good thing Zenia had the courage to tell us she saw Carter around the backpacks too. Otherwise, Justin wouldn't even be on the team anymore."

Coach puts a hand on each of our shoulders. "Your brother was just about to be asked to leave tonight, you know, Shauna," he says. "I don't really believe he had anything to do with the theft. I still have faith in him."

"Thanks, Coach," Shauna says, smiling. "So do I."

I can't help but think how much worse it could have been for Justin.

"Come on. Let's go check on Zenia and my brother," says Shauna, and we hurry back into the noisy gym.

Zenia is talking to Kat, Paige and Isabel as Justin pretends to slow dance with an invisible partner. I *so* wish I could be laughing with the other kids who are watching him. I wish everything could go back to normal between me and my friends. I wish I could vanish into thin air. Kat is staring at me. I can see her expression in the light from the hall door. I turn away quickly. What are they saying about me? Why do friendships have to be so complicated?

I glance around for Shauna, but she's dancing with Zack now. I feel so alone. I lean against the wall and wish the night was over and I was in my bed. I close my eyes tight and sigh. Then there's a tap on my shoulder.

When I open my eyes, Kat is staring at me with a weird expression on her face. Paige and Isabel are behind her with wobbly half smiles. Now what? Kat wraps me up in a big hug and squeezes me hard.

"Huh? What's going on?" I say.

"Zenia told us what you did for Shauna. To help her brother. I feel so lame for treating you the way I have the last couple of days." She pauses and gulps. "And for letting you beat me. That was the dumbest thing ever."

"I still can't believe you did that," I say. "It sucks. I thought I'd caught up to you."

"Look, let's talk at practice tomorrow. We have to save our friendship, Maddy."

Kat's bottom lip quivers, and she blinks quickly. But I'm still bummed that she let me win.

"Okay," I say. "We'll sort it out tomorrow." I give her a quick hug back.

Paige and Isabel swoop in. We have this crazy group hug, and they apologize for acting like jerks. I'm so relieved, I can't even speak. I return the tangled hug as best I can. And I try my best to believe that somehow everything will work out.

chapter twenty-one

Kids start trickling out of the gym shortly before the dance officially ends at 10:30. A group of us walk home together, winding our way through the side streets. The farther we get from the school, the smaller the crowd gets. Soon it's just me, Shauna, Kat, Justin and Zenia. I'll bet Shauna wishes Matt was here.

I stop dead when I spot a police cruiser up ahead, parked beside the road.

The lights are on inside, and broken glass glitters on the road. Three kids are crammed into the back, but I can't see their faces. A police officer in the front seat is writing something down. Another officer stands beside the car talking to someone who looks up when he hears us. Our eyes meet, and I freeze. I spin around and sprint home, ignoring the shouts of my friends behind me.

I don't quit running until I reach my front door. I stop to catch my breath before bursting inside. I can't let Mom or Abuelo see me like this, or they'll know something is wrong. Sooner or later they'll learn Matt was nabbed by the cops. But I'm not ready to tell them yet. Right now, I just want to hide, to pretend it never happened.

The hallway and living room are dark, thank god. I scuffle down the hall to my bedroom and softly close the door. I flop on the bed and let my tears flow. I'm not sure how long I lie there before I finally fall asleep.

A while later, a light tapping at my bedroom door nudges me awake. I check the clock. It's only 1:00, but it feels much later than that. I pull a pillow over my head. If it's Mom or Abuelo looking for Matt,

I'm not ready to face them right now. A finger pokes me hard in the middle of my back.

"Maddy, you awake?"

I roll over. In the light from the hallway, I see my brother's face. And I have to stop myself from slapping it.

"Why aren't you in jail, you jerk?" I manage to blurt before ducking under the covers so I won't have to look at him.

"Because I didn't do anything," he says.

I'm not sure I've heard him correctly. I lift the blanket to look at him. "What? You didn't?"

"Yeah, you heard me, Maddy. I didn't do anything. Well, anything bad. But I kind of did do *something*."

"You mean you weren't getting arrested when I saw you with that cop?"

"Of course not! I was on my way home from work, trying to make it to the gym before the dance ended. I ran into Carter and his friends. They were acting like total losers, trying to push down a stop sign, sitting on parked cars, breaking beer bottles on the road. I tried to stop them."

"They got kicked out of the dance for acting like jackasses, you know," I say.

"No doubt! So then this cop car came flying out of nowhere. I guess it looked like I was part of it all. Until they understood what was going on. They let me go once I explained I was trying to stop them," Matt says. "Carter tried to tell them I was there all along. He's such a knob!"

"I saw those guys in the backseat. But I took off when I saw you with the cop. I thought you were involved with Carter and his friends. I just thought the worst when I saw what was happening, Matt!"

I reach out and give him a quick hug. Then I tell him how Zenia came through for Justin at the dance.

"We actually did it. We stopped Justin from getting into trouble!"

My brother shakes his head. "Wow, can you believe everything that has happened tonight, Maddy?"

"No kidding," I say and pull the blankets back over my head to go to sleep.

I sleep hard after Matt leaves my room and don't wake until my clock radio blasts hip-hop at 9:00 Saturday morning.

Before I even open my eyes, I smell fresh coffee and hear home fries sizzling in a pan. Abuelo likes to give his two athletes a good breakfast. What a relief that I won't have to face Mom and Abuelo with an awful story about their Mateo this morning. In fact, there's no need to tell them anything, since nothing bad happened to either one of us.

I stay in bed for a moment, thankful that things turned out last night. Carter and his crew are in for a huge wake-up call. And Kat and I are going to work things out at practice today. This morning, I actually do feel a bit like Little Miss Sunshine!

In the kitchen, Mom, Abuelo and Matt are gathered around the table. Mom and Abuelo lean forward, listening to Matt tell them about last night.

"Oh, there she is, the other hero," Abuelo says as I slip into a chair.

"Hero? How am I a hero? What did I do? Matt's the hero—he's the one who was trying to stop those idiots last night."

"Ah, but you. You stopped Justin from being there with them," Abuelo says, smiling.

"That was a good plan," Mom says. "You two. What busy lives you lead. So much going on all the time. I'm so proud of both of you."

Matt has a half smile on his face. I decide he's been hiding his secret life way too long.

"Mom, Abuelo, how about if Matt and I take you out for dinner tonight? Our treat," I say. Matt's eyes grow wide.

"Dinner? Really? You mean I don't have to cook tonight?" Abuelo says.

Mom looks baffled. "Where do you want to take us for dinner, Maddy?"

"It's a surprise," I say. "You'll have to wait and see."

"And you're coming too, Mateo?" Abuelo asks. "Even though you're so busy?"

"Yeah," Matt says. "But I'll have to meet you there, okay?"

Matt winks at me. I inhale Abuelo's delicious breakfast so I can hustle over to the track and practice. I've made a decision.

I am going to win on Monday!

chapter twenty-two

On the way to the track, Matt and I talk about our dinner plans. He's worried about how Mom and Abuelo will react when they see him behind the counter at Burger King.

"What if they get mad at me," he says. "What if they don't like the burgers? What if they don't want me to have a job because it cuts into my school and sports time? What if they don't think I can handle it?"

"Quit worrying, Matt," I say. "You've been doing it for a few months already.

Trust me, they'll be proud of you. And the burgers will be the best Abuelo has ever tasted, because you cooked them!"

Matt nudges my shoulder. "Sure hope you're right, Maddy."

I can't help thinking, *I sure hope so too*.

Everyone is already at the track when we arrive. Everyone except Carter and his friends, of course. Justin and Zenia are running side by side. Maybe last night turned out better than they expected. Shauna's doing laps and gives me a thumbs-up as she passes. Kat flashes me a peace sign from across the track. But there's still some tension hanging between us.

We've just started warming up when Coach Reeves appears. Coach never shows up for Saturday morning practices. As soon as he blows his whistle, we all hurry over.

He's more somber than usual. "I'm sure many of you have already heard about what happened after the dance last night. Am I right?" His hands are on his hips, and one foot slowly taps the ground.

We all nod.

"Carter will be out of commission for the rest of the season. He and a couple of his friends were picked up by the police last night after getting kicked out of the dance. There's something else you should be aware of—Justin Halstead had nothing to do with the theft last Saturday. His name has been cleared thanks to someone brave enough to come forward and tell us what really happened."

When I glance over at Zenia, she gives me a subtle smile. I think she's finally forgiven me for not helping her when Carter and his friends pushed her around.

Coach's voice becomes more serious, and his eyes lock on Justin. "Would you like to add anything, Justin?"

Justin clears his throat. Zenia gives him a little nudge, and he nods. "I just want to say sorry to all of you for acting like such a jerk lately on the track and in school. That's over. It's all about the team now. I promise."

Zenia smiles at me again, and I give her a thumbs-up. Shauna is standing next to

Matt and beaming. Everything has turned out better than I expected.

Practice goes really well. It's as if now that our minds are free of the problems that have been hanging over us, we're in top form. Before leaving, Coach told us he'll be making his decisions after Monday's practice.

Kat and I don't even try to race each other that morning. I still can't believe she's been letting me win all along just for the sake of our friendship. Halfway through practice, she walks over to me wearing a forced smile. I know it's time to get this settled once and for all. If I can't beat her on the track, I decide I'm going to beat her to the punch.

"So why *did* you do it?" I ask as we walk over to sit under a tree away from the rest of the team. "It doesn't make any sense. I dealt with your wins last year. I would have been able to again this year, you know."

Kat heaves a huge sigh and shakes her head. "With so many other kids on the team this year, I was afraid of losing you as my closest friend. So I let you win half my races. Just so we'd keep laughing about it instead of competing seriously with each other. I wanted us to stay close. And in the end, I really did want Coach to make the decision so it wouldn't be me beating you. So you wouldn't resent me."

"Wow," I say. "Kat, we're best friends. But it's okay to have *other* friends too."

"Yeah," she says. "I finally figured that out. But it took Zenia to convince me. She told me how you helped Shauna and Justin. You're a way better friend than I am."

"That's not true," I say. "And here's how you can prove it."

And that's when I tell Kat what she can do on Monday to save our friendship.

By Monday morning, my head is swimming with all the crazy things that happened on the weekend. Nothing was more hilarious than Abuelo telling the whole restaurant that his grandson is a top chef and cooked the burger himself. Which cracked up everyone who heard him! Mom and Abuelo were incredibly proud of my brother. And Matt was relieved they finally knew about his job. He even thanked me.

After school on Monday, Kat, Zenia, Shauna and I, and some of the other runners, crouch at the starting line. Everyone is intense and focused. The winner of this race will represent the school in the 100-meter sprint. The four runners with the best times will make up the relay team. The fifth will be the sub. Ahead of us, the finish line is a blur of color. A crowd has gathered to watch. Everyone is anxious to find out how this will end.

My toes press into the starting block, and my heart hammers. My eyes are focused straight ahead. The other girls crouched along the starting line don't matter right now. This is between me and Kat. No more giving up races on purpose. This time, I want a real competition. I want to find out if I really can beat her.

"Set!" Coach yells.

My whole body tenses. Every muscle is waiting to snap.

Bang! The pistol goes off, and we churn up the track, sprinting for the finish line. I blast forward as fast as I can, powered by adrenaline and hours of training. I push harder than I ever have. I imagine my legs as a couple of pumping pistons. The steady beat of running shoes pounding against crushed gravel and my heart thumping in my ears are the only things I hear.

I am determined to beat Kat, my best friend.

I sprint across the finish line with my arms in the air. Kat has hers in the air too. Our eyes meet.

Coach yells, "We have a winner!"

Now, at last, we'll know.

"Congratulations, Shauna. You won. Zenia, you're third. And you two..."

Kat looks as shocked as I feel.

Coach smiles. "You two tied for second place."

Deb Loughead is the author of more than twenty-five books for children and young adults. Deb conducts workshops and readings at schools, festivals and conferences across the country. She has written and directed children's plays and taught creative writing classes. Back in her youth, she was a sprinter, as well as the anchor, for her school relay team. Nowadays she prefers walking her dog. Deb lives with her family in Toronto, Ontario.